Anansi
and the
Sheep

by Adam Bushnell and Nuno Alexandre Vieira

W
FRANKLIN WATTS
LONDON•SYDNEY

In a time long ago, there lived Anansi.

He was no ordinary spider.

He was a spider who liked to help others.

One day, Anansi was busy building a web

in a tree near a farm, when he saw

a sad sheep.

"What's the matter?" asked Anansi.

"I'm so hungry," replied the sheep.

Anansi looked surprised.

"But can't you eat the grass?" he said.

The sheep shook his head. "No,"
he replied. "There hasn't been any rain
for a long time. The grass is dried up and
the pond has no water. I wish I could leave
and find a nice, green field to live in."

Anansi knew he could help the sheep find
a new field to live in. So he shot out
his web threads to make a ramp,
and helped the sheep cross over
the fence.

Just then, the farmer came out of
the barn. He looked very angry.
"Stop, thief!" he shouted at Anansi.
Anansi and the sheep ran away
as quickly as they could.

Anansi and the sheep ran and ran.

They ran so fast that they did not look

where they were going.

They ran straight into a lion.

The lion roared and showed his teeth.

Anansi looked around. He saw lots of

heavy, ripe mangos hanging in the tree

above the lion. This gave Anansi an idea.

"Do not eat us!" cried Anansi. "The sky is falling! You must run away!"

The lion looked up.

Anansi quickly picked up a rock and threw it at a mango. The mango fell to the ground with a crash.

The lion thought the sky really was falling. He screamed with fright and ran away.

Anansi and the sheep ran and ran.

They both wanted to get far away from

the lion.

But then, they ran straight into a cheetah.

The cheetah growled and licked his lips.

"Do not eat us!" cried Anansi, pointing to the sky. "The sky is falling! You must run away!"

Anansi threw a rock while the cheetah wasn't looking. He knocked down a few limes behind the cheetah. The cheetah, too, thought the sky was falling. He screamed with fright and ran away.

Anansi and the sheep ran and ran.

By now they were too tired to notice

what was ahead of them.

They ran straight into a panther.

The panther snarled and snapped his jaws.

"Do not eat us!" shouted Anansi, pointing up. "The sky is falling! You must run away!"

The panther looked up.

Anansi used a rock to knock down a bunch of bananas.

The panther heard the bananas crashing down behind him. He screamed with fright and ran away.

Anansi and the sheep ran and ran. Finally, they came to a field of nice, green grass.

"Here you are," said Anansi. "This can be your new home and you can eat as much of this nice, green grass as you like."

The sheep ate and ate.

When evening came, Anansi made a web up in a tree.

He helped the sheep climb up and they both went to sleep in the large web.

Just then, the lion, cheetah and panther came along. They sat next to the tree. "A spider and a sheep told me the sky was falling," the lion grumbled. "They tricked me."

"The same thing happened to me," the cheetah growled.

"And to me," the panther snarled.

"If we see those two again, we should eat them up!" roared the lion.

Anansi looked at the sheep and whispered,

"Keep very quiet."

"But, they'll eat us if they see us up here,"

said the sheep. He was so frightened that

he began to shake.

"Stop shaking," said Anansi. "You'll fall out!"

But the sheep couldn't stop shaking.
All of a sudden, he fell out of the web and
hit the ground with a thud.

"Oh no! The sky really is falling!"

screamed the lion.

"A cloud just fell from the sky!"

cried the cheetah.

"Let's get out of here!" yelled the panther.

The three animals ran away as fast as

they could.

Anansi and the sheep smiled at each other,
then settled back down to sleep.

When they woke the next morning,
they looked out over the nice, green field.
"Do you like it here?" Anansi asked.
"Oh yes!" cried the sheep. "It's much nicer
here than on the dried-up farm. Thank you
for helping me."

Anansi hugged his new friend, then set off to find more animals to help.

The sheep stayed in the field. He ate all the grass he wanted. And in that nice, green field he lived happily ever after.

Story order

Look at these 5 pictures and captions.
Put the pictures in the right order
to retell the story.

1

Anansi tricks the lion, cheetah and panther.

2

The cats are scared by the sheep falling.

Anansi and the sheep come to a new field.

Anansi helps the sheep leave the farm.

The sheep is happy.

Independent Reading

This series is designed to provide an opportunity for your child to read on their own. These notes are written for you to help your child choose a book and to read it independently.

In school, your child's teacher will often be using reading books which have been banded to support the process of learning to read. Use the book band colour your child is reading in school to help you make a good choice. *Anansi and the Sheep* is a good choice for children reading at Purple Band in their classroom to read independently.

The aim of independent reading is to read this book with ease, so that your child enjoys the story and relates it to their own experiences.

About the book
Anansi is a spider who likes to help others. In this story, he helps a sad sheep find a new home while tricking three very hungry predators!

Before reading
Help your child to learn how to make good choices by asking:
"Why did you choose this book? Why do you think you will enjoy it?"
Look at the cover together and ask: "What do you think the story will be about?" Ask your child to think of what they already know about the story context. Then ask your child to read the title aloud. Ask:
"Have you read any other Anansi stories? Do you think Anansi and the sheep will be friends or enemies? Why?"
Remind your child that they can sound out the letters to make a word if they get stuck.
Decide together whether your child will read the story independently or read it aloud to you.

During reading

Remind your child of what they know and what they can do independently. If reading aloud, support your child if they hesitate or ask for help by telling the word. If reading to themselves, remind your child that they can come and ask for your help if stuck.

After reading

Support comprehension by asking your child to tell you about the story. Use the story order puzzle to encourage your child to retell the story in the right sequence, in their own words. The correct sequence can be found on the next page.

Help your child think about the messages in the book that go beyond the story and ask: "Who was the cleverest character in the story? How did he use that cleverness to be helpful?"

Give your child a chance to respond to the story: "What was your favourite part? Why?"

Extending learning

Help your child think more about the inferences in the story by asking: "Why do you think the big animals thought the sheep was a cloud? What part of the situation confused them?"

In the classroom, your child's teacher may be teaching different kinds of sentences. There are many examples in this book that you could look at with your child, including statements, commands and questions. Find these together and point out how the end punctuation can help us decide what kind of sentence it is.

Franklin Watts
First published in Great Britain in 2020
by The Watts Publishing Group

Copyright © The Watts Publishing Group 2020
All rights reserved.

Series Editors: Jackie Hamley, Melanie Palmer and Grace Glendinning
Series Advisors: Dr Sue Bodman and Glen Franklin
Series Designers: Peter Scoulding and Cathryn Gilbert

A CIP catalogue record for this book is
available from the British Library.

ISBN 978 1 4451 7173 9 (hbk)
ISBN 978 1 4451 7174 6 (pbk)
ISBN 978 1 4451 7295 8 (library ebook)

Printed in China

Franklin Watts
An imprint of
Hachette Children's Group
Part of The Watts Publishing Group
Carmelite House
50 Victoria Embankment
London EC4Y 0DZ

An Hachette UK Company
www.hachette.co.uk

www.reading-champion.co.uk

Answer to Story order: 4, 1, 3, 2, 5